P9-EMH-002

City Green

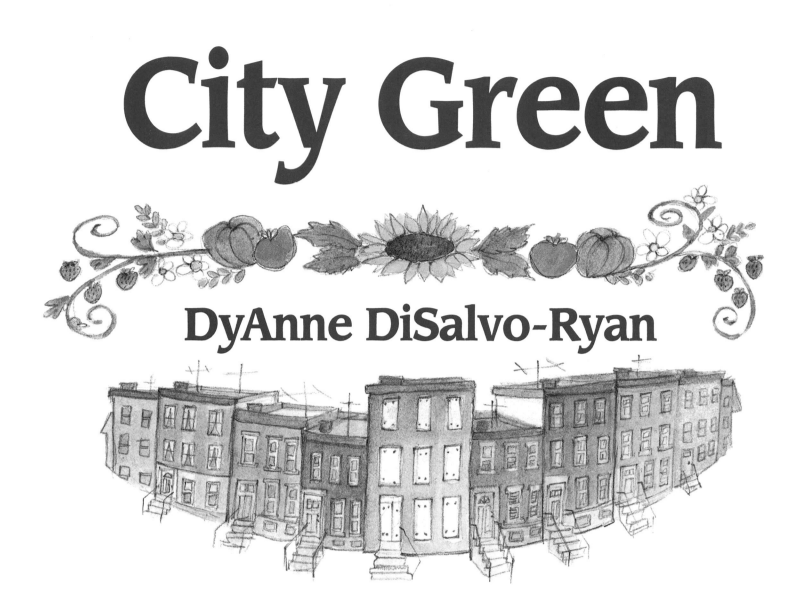

DyAnne DiSalvo-Ryan

Morrow Junior Books   New York

For my mother,
who can listen to my stories
and fry eggplants at the
same time.

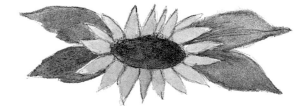

The author would like to acknowledge the American Community Gardening Association,
Philadelphia Green, Operation GreenThumb, the Point Breeze Federation,
and the Garden of Union for their time and cooperation.
Special thanks to my editor, Meredith Charpentier,
and my agent, Jane Feder, for all their weeding and watering.

A portion of the author's royalties will be donated to the American Community Gardening Association.

Watercolors, pencil, and crayons were used for the full-color illustrations. The text type is 14-point Leawood Book.

Library of Congress Cataloging-in-Publication Data
DiSalvo-Ryan, DyAnne.   City green / DyAnne DiSalvo-Ryan.   p.   cm.
Summary: Marcy and Miss Rosa start a campaign to clean up an empty lot and turn it into a community garden.
ISBN 0-688-12786-X (trade). — ISBN 0-688-12787-8 (library)
[1. Community gardens—Fiction.   2. Gardens—Fiction.   3. City and town life—Fiction.]   I. Title.
PZ7.D6224Th   1994   [E]—dc20   93-27117   CIP   AC
18 19 20 PC 40 39 38 37 36

There used to be a building right here on this lot. It was three floors up and down, an empty building nailed up shut for as long as I could remember. My friend Miss Rosa told me Old Man Hammer used to live there—some other neighbors too. But when I asked him about that, he only hollered, "Scram."

Old Man Hammer, hard as nails.

Last year two people from the city came by, dressed in suits and holding papers. They said, "This building is unsafe. It will have to be torn down."

By winter a crane with a wrecking ball was parked outside. Mama gathered everyone to watch from our front window. In three slow blows that building was knocked into a heap of pieces. Then workers took the rubble away in a truck and filled the hole with dirt.

Now this block looks like a big smile with one tooth missing. Old Man Hammer sits on his stoop and shakes his head. "Look at that piece of junk land on a city block," Old Man Hammer says. "Once that building could've been saved. But nobody even tried."

And every day when I pass this lot it makes me sad to see it. Every single day.

Then spring comes, and right on schedule Miss Rosa starts cleaning her coffee cans. Miss Rosa and I keep coffee cans outside our windowsills. Every year we buy two packets of seeds at the hardware store—sometimes marigolds, sometimes zinnias, and one time we tried tomatoes. We go to the park, scoop some dirt, and fill up the cans halfway.

This time Old Man Hammer stops us on the way to the park. "This good for nothin' lot has plenty of dirt right here," he says.

Then all at once I look at Miss Rosa. And she is smiling back at me. "A *lot* of dirt," Miss Rosa says.

"Like one big coffee can," I say.

That's when we decide to do something about this lot.

Quick as a wink I'm digging away, already thinking of gardens and flowers. But Old Man Hammer shakes his finger. "You can't dig more dirt than that. This lot is city property."

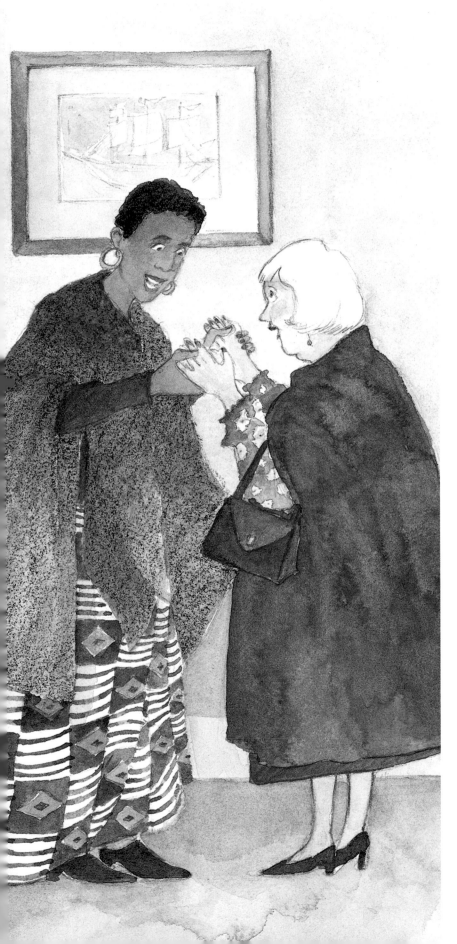

Miss Rosa and I go to see Mr. Bennett. He used to work for the city. "I seem to remember a program," he says, "that lets people rent empty lots."

That's how Miss Rosa and I form a group of people from our block. We pass around a petition that says: WE WANT TO LEASE THIS LOT. In less than a week we have plenty of names.

"Sign with us?" I ask Old Man Hammer.

"I'm not signin' nothin'," he says. "And nothin' is what's gonna happen."

But something did.

The next week, a bunch of us take a bus to city hall. We walk up the steps to the proper office and hand the woman our list. She checks her files and types some notes and makes some copies. "That will be one dollar, please."

We rent the lot from the city that day. It was just as simple as that.

Saturday morning I'm up with the sun and looking at this lot. My mama looks out too. "Marcy," she says, and hugs me close. "Today I'm helping you and Rosa."

After shopping, Mama empties her grocery bags and folds them flat to carry under her arm. "Come on, Mrs. B.," Mama tells her friend. "We're going to clear this lot."

Then what do you know but my brother comes along. My brother is tall and strong. At first, he scratches his neck and shakes his head just like Old Man Hammer. But Mama smiles and says, "None of that here!" So all day long he piles junk in those bags and carries them to the curb.

Now, this time of day is early. Neighbors pass by and see what we're doing. Most say, "We want to help too." They have a little time to spare. Then this one calls that one and that one calls another.

"Come on and help," I call to Old Man Hammer.

"I'm not helpin' nobody," he hollers. "You're all wastin' your time."

Sour grapes my mama'd say, and sour grapes is right.

Just before supper, when we are good and hungry, my mama looks around this lot. "Marcy," she says, "you're making something happen here."

Next day the city drops off tools like rakes and brooms, and a Dumpster for trash. Now there's even more neighbors to help. Miss Rosa, my brother, and I say "Good morning" to Old Man Hammer, but Old Man Hammer just waves like he's swatting a fly.

"Why is Old Man Hammer so mean and cranky these days?" my brother asks.

"Maybe he's really sad," I tell him. "Maybe he misses his building."

"That rotten old building?" My brother shrugs. "He should be happy the city tore down that mess."

"Give him time," Miss Rosa says. "Good things take time."

Mr. Bennett brings wood—old slats he's saved—and nails in a cup. "I knew all along I saved them for something," he says. "This wood's good wood."

Then Mr. Rocco from two houses down comes, carrying two cans of paint. "I'll never use these," he says. "The color's too bright. But here, this lot could use some brightening up."

Well, anyone can tell with all the excitement that something is going on. And everyone has an idea about what to plant—strawberries, carrots, lettuce, and more. Tulips and daisies, petunias, and more! Sonny turns the dirt over with a snow shovel. Even Leslie's baby tries to dig with a spoon.

For lunch, Miss Rosa brings milk and jelly and bread and spreads a beach towel where the junk is cleared. By the end of the day a fence is built and painted as bright as the sun.

Later, Mama kisses my cheek and closes my bedroom door. By the streetlights I see Old Man Hammer come down his steps to open the gate and walk to the back of this lot. He bends down quick, sprinkling something from his pocket and covering it over with dirt.

In the morning I tell my brother. "Oh, Marcy," he says. "You're dreaming. You're wishing too hard."

But I know what I saw, and I tell my mama, "Old Man Hammer's planted some seeds."

Right after breakfast, I walk to the back of this lot. And there it is—a tiny raised bed of soil. It is neat and tidy, just like the rows we've planted. Now I know for sure that Old Man Hammer planted something. So I pat the soil for good luck and make a little fence to keep the seeds safe.

Every day I go for a look inside our garden lot. Other neighbors stop in too. One day Mrs. Wells comes by. "This is right where my grandmother's bedroom used to be," she says. "That's why I planted my flowers there."

I feel sad when I hear that. With all the digging and planting and weeding and watering, I'd forgotten about the building that had been on this lot. Old Man Hammer had lived there too. I go to the back, where he planted his seeds. I wonder if this was the place where his room used to be.

I look down. Beside my feet, some tiny stems are sprouting. Old Man Hammer's seeds have grown! I run to his stoop. "Come with me!" I beg, tugging at his hand. "You'll want to see."

I walk him past the hollyhocks, the daisies, the peppers, the rows of lettuce. I show him the strawberries that I planted. When Old Man Hammer sees his little garden bed, his sour grapes turn sweet. "Marcy, child." He shakes his head. "This lot was good for nothin'. Now it's nothin' but good," he says.

Soon summertime comes, and this lot really grows. It fills with vegetables, herbs, and flowers. And way in the back, taller than anything else, is a beautiful patch of yellow sunflowers. Old Man Hammer comes every day. He sits in the sun, eats his lunch, and sometimes comes back with supper.

Nobody knows how the sunflowers came—not Leslie, my brother, or Miss Rosa. Not Mr. Bennett, or Sonny, or anyone else. But Old Man Hammer just sits there smiling at me. We know whose flowers they are.

Starting a Community Garden

All across America people have joined together to turn ugly lots into beautiful gardens. You may not imagine that you can do it—but you *can*. If there is already a community garden in your neighborhood, ask your neighbors how they got started. But if you are the first on your block to "make something happen," this is what you can do:

1. Find an interested grown-up who wants to help you: a parent or guardian, a teacher, a librarian, or a neighbor.

2. Find out the address of the lot. This is very important. You may have to talk to neighbors or look at the address of the buildings next door. Example: The lot I am interested in is on Main Street. It is between 75 Main Street and 81 Main Street.

3. While you are finding out the address of the lot, get in touch with the local gardening program in your area (see end of this note). Say that you are interested in starting a garden. Since every city is different, your local program will be able to steer you in the right direction.

4. Find out who the owner is. The Department of Records at your local city hall can help. Look in the telephone book for the address of city hall in your area.

5. If the lot is owned by the city, the people at city hall can help you get permission to use the lot. Usually there is a small fee. If the lot is owned by an individual person or group, you will need to get permission from that person or group to use the lot.

6. Once you get permission to use the lot, it's yours to name!

There are hundreds of gardening programs that are ready to help community gardeners with information, soil, seeds, fencing, and more.

To find out the community gardening program that is nearest you, write to:

American Community Gardening Association
100 North 20th Street, 5th Floor
Philadelphia, PA 19103

Community gardens bring people together. Join the work and join the fun!